W9-BMA-427

Guess Again!
Riddle Poems

Lillian Morrison

Illustrated by

Christy Hale

AUGUST HOUSE
LittleFolk

LITTLE ROCK

For Liana and Daniela—LM

For my godson, Ian Stafford Wilson—CH

A Note from the Author

Each poem here is a little rhythmic puzzle-package with an answer inside. It is up to you, the reader, to "open" each one and solve it by discovering the subject of the poem. If you listen carefully to the words and pay close attention to the pictures, this should not be too hard. Just rack your brain and... guess again! If you still don't come up with an answer, turn the page, look once more, and you will find it.

Riddles are fun because they make you think and see likenesses you haven't seen before. Sometimes there is a trick in the words, and there's always a clue in the picture. And once you know the answers, you can enjoy stumping your friends and family with these riddles as well as some of your own. —LM

Text © 2006 by Lillian Morrison. Illustrations © 2006 by Christy Hale. All rights reserved. This book, or parts thereof, may not be reproduced in any form without permission. Published 2006 by August House Publishers, Inc., P.O. Box 3223, Little Rock, Arkansas 72203, 501-372-5450 www.augusthouse.com. Book design by Christy Hale. Manufactured in Korea. 10 9 8 7 6 5 4 3 2 1

Library of Congress Cataloging-in-Publication Data Morrison, Lillian. Guess again! : riddle poems / Lillian Morrison; illustrated by Christy Hale. p. cm. ISBN-13: 978-0-87483-730-8   ISBN-10: 0-87483-730-8 (alk. paper) 1. Children's poetry, American. 2. Riddles, Juvenile. I. Hale, Christy, ill. II. Title. PS3563.08747G84   2006   811'.54—dc22 2005052620 The paper used in this publication meets the minimum requirements of the American National Standards for Information Sciences—Permanence of Paper for Printed Library Materials, ANSI.48–1984.

Easy to open, no need to unlock it.
Sometimes it's small enough to carry in your pocket.
But when it is open it can carry you
through fascinating spaces like a far-flying rocket.

A book

Shaped like a walnut, doesn't weigh much
yet gives birth to worlds. Can you imagine such?
Dreams ride there. Poems hide there.

The brain

At first I am hard and small
without any taste at all.
Then it's ricochet, richochet, puff!
I'm an edible piece of fluff.

Popcorn

They have tongues
but they can't talk with you.
They have no legs
but they can walk with you.

Sneakers

I chewed and I blew.
It was the thing to do.
Now I can't get it off my nose
and I can't get it off my shoe.

Bubblegum

They come out into the air
because you've pushed them there.
You may wish you never had
but they're there for good or bad.

The words you've spoken

At times it sings or softly speaks
At times it bangs and shouts or shrieks,
yet it can take you to wondrous places
as it sits against a wall making faces.

The TV

Something brilliant flashes by,
then it grumbles in the sky.
Sometimes it's an awful rumbling.
It sounds as though the world is crumbling.

Lightning and thunder

It's in the river

but not in the lake.

It's in the raindrop

but not the snowflake.

The letter R

Here come tiger down the track—
big white eye and a mile-long back.
Through the dark he makes his run
looking for the sky and sun.

A train

Where it comes from
there's no knowing.
You can kill it
but it keeps on going.

Time

It's not a planet out in space,
but it has a moon.
You can find it near your face
each time you lift your spoon.

Your fingernail

It has no corners
yet it's not exactly round.
You buy it by the dozen
instead of by the pound.

I'm still
hungry.

An egg

It's cold and it drips.
You put it to your lips.
It's better not to bite.
Just lick it with delight.

Ice cream

I came one summer day
upon a lovely scene:
Sky above, sky below
and no land in between.

A lake with reflections

It stands straight and tall
against a blue sky
and lifts arms in welcome
to birds that stop by.

A tree

Their sides are sometimes rough,
their heads held very high.
Broad, solid on the ground,
they push up to the sky.

Mountains

They'll support you where you stand.
They can bend at your command.
All have caps. Some have a dimple.
Can you guess? It's really simple.

Knees

This is the riddle I wish to pose:
It comes and goes, comes and goes.
It licks your heels, nibbles your toes,
erases your footsteps, and away it flows.

The ocean

It sinks in the ocean but doesn't drown.
The next day you see it painting the town.

The sun

It sweeps the town
without brush or broom.
If you open your window,
it will sweep your room.

The wind

You turn it and punch it,
you smoothe it and scrunch it.
At times you might heave it
at friends in a fight.
Yet it's there for your comfort
every night.

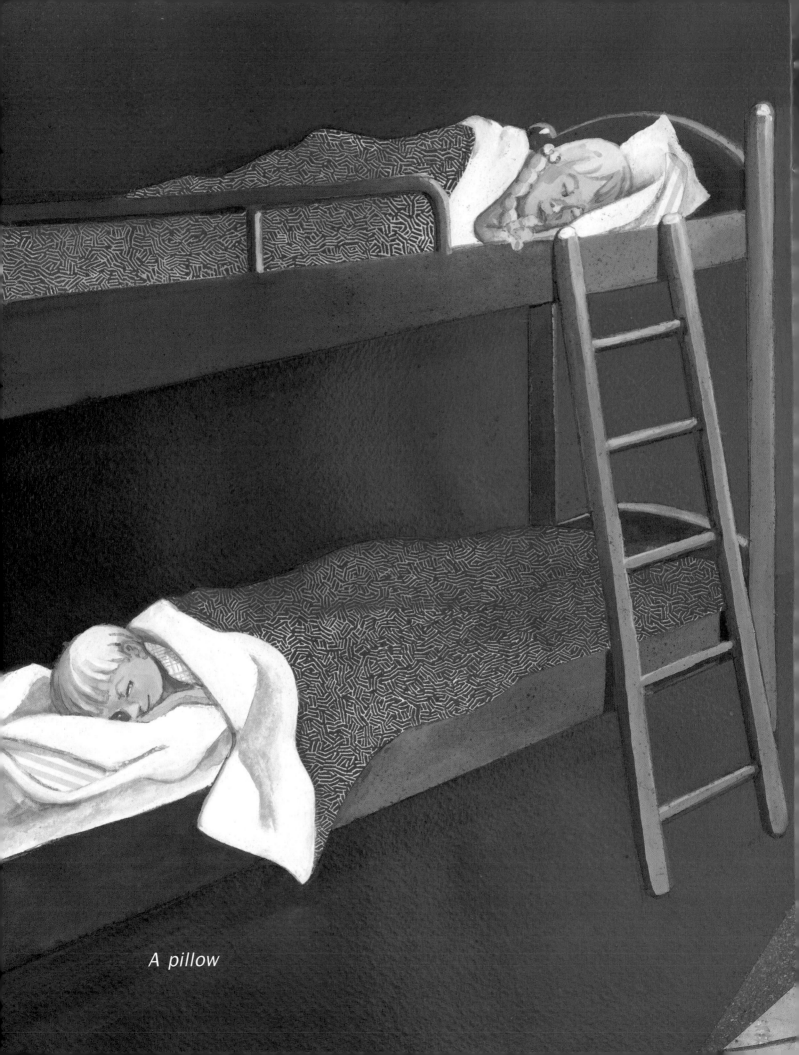

A pillow

At night it sees
through slits of trees
and softly streams
its laser beams
onto your bedroom floor
as if to send a message
for sweet dreams.

The moon